Joshua's Desert Diary

Written by Ros Woodman
Illustrated by James P Smith
Designed by Hazel Scrimshire

CF4•K

It's not often that you're allowed to read someone else's diary, but you have a chance to do just that with this book. If Joshua had written a diary, this is what it might have been like. It all starts with an adventure in Egypt, when a man called Moses came to the Hebrew camp with some exciting news.

Dear Diary,

I'm so excited! Our wonderful God has seen how badly we slaves are treated by the Egyptians. He is going to help us. A man named Moses has been chosen to lead the Hebrew people out of Egypt. He was looking after sheep by Mount Horeb when he saw a bush on fire that wasn't burning up! When he hurried over, a voice called him from the bush, 'Do not come any closer. Take off your sandals. You are standing on holy ground.'

It was God. Moses was so afraid he hid his face. God said that he had seen the suffering of our people. He was going to take us to a land flowing with milk and honey. Moses was to tell the people that I AM had sent him.

God then told Moses to throw his stick onto the ground and it became a snake! When he caught it by the tail, it became a stick again. When Moses put his hand inside his coat it came out covered with a skin infection. He did it again, and his hand was back to normal. This was all part of a plan to make the people believe Moses. Moses has also been told to ask Pharaoh to let our people go into the desert and offer sacrifices to God. However, Moses says he can't speak well so God has chosen his brother, Aaron, to speak for him. Moses and Aaron have spoken with our leaders and shown them miracles. The leaders believe them. Everyone is praising God.

Joshua

Dear Diary,

Pharaoh is very angry. Moses and Aaron gave him God's message and now he is making the Hebrew people work harder than ever. Pharaoh says we are lazy. Our people are blaming Moses and Aaron.

But Moses and Aaron have seen Pharaoh again. Aaron threw down his stick and it became a snake. However, the magicians in Pharaoh's court were able to do the same thing. But Aaron's snake gobbled up all the rest.

Pharaoh still won't listen to God.

Then the other day Moses waited for Pharaoh to come down to the river and asked him again to let us go. When he said no, Moses hit the river with his stick. We could hardly believe it. The great river Nile turned to blood. So did the water in the whole of Egypt.

The fish died and the smell was terrible. After the Nile was turned to blood – then the frogs started to arrive. They were jumping on people, crawling on the beds and in the ovens. Nowhere was frog-free. Aaron simply stretched his stick over the waters and out they came. He isn't the only one – Pharaoh's magicians have created even more!

But praise God! Pharaoh has told Moses we can leave if he sorts out the frogs.

Joshua

Dear Diary,

I've got some good news and bad news. Good news first. God has made the frogs die. They are piled in heaps throughout Egypt and the smell is dreadful – but the bad news is worse than that.

Pharaoh has broken his promise. We are still slaves. So there are more plagues to come.

Aaron hit the dust with his stick and a swarm of gnats came up out of it. This time the magicians couldn't copy it. They said it was caused by God. Everyone was itching and scratching – even the animals. It didn't have an effect on Pharaoh, so God sent another plague – flies!

The buzzing was unbelievable – the Egyptians hated it. The flies were everywhere – laying eggs in the food and crawling on the babies. It's amazing though – in Goshen where we slaves live, I didn't see a single one. Anyway, Pharaoh called Moses and the flies have gone. Perhaps he's finally agreed to free us?

Joshua

Dear Diary,

It was a mistake to think that Pharaoh would change his mind. Moses says that God has hardened Pharaoh's heart. Now there is more trouble.

There has been a terrible plague on the animals in Egypt. Horses, donkeys, camels, sheep and cows have died – except for our own in Goshen. Then Moses threw soot in the air and terrible boils broke out on the Egyptians. They were in agony. Even the magicians had them.

Last night after Pharaoh had refused Moses again, God sent the worst hail storm Egypt has ever had. It didn't fall on us in Goshen, but we could hear the thunder and see the lightening. Today, the land is in a sorry state. The fields are flattened and trees are stripped. Some of the crops have been destroyed. How much longer before Pharaoh lets us go?

Joshua

Dear Diary,

A terrible event is about to happen. At midnight tonight, every first-born Egyptian son will die. Then, at last, Pharaoh will let us go.

God gave special instructions. Each household had to take a perfect year old sheep or goat; it had to be male. The animal then had to be killed and the blood smeared onto the tops and sides of the door frames. We have to do this as only then will our own first-born be saved.

It feels strange. Tonight is our last in Egypt as slaves. The animals we killed were roasted earlier. They were eaten with bitter herbs and bread made without yeast. God said that we were to eat quickly, with our coats tucked into our belts, sandals on our feet, and a stick in our hands.

It is late now and people are whispering nervously. Soon we will leave. I am watching and waiting.

Joshua

Dear Diary,

It has happened just as God said. The sound of weeping and wailing was terrible as the first-born died. Pharaoh told us to leave. The Egyptians gave us gold, silver and clothing. 'Hurry up and leave,' they said. 'Or we will all die.'

As we travelled towards the Red Sea God sent a pillar of cloud to lead us during the day and a pillar of fire by night. But now bad news has reached us. Pharaoh has changed his mind and is chasing us with his army. The only way to escape is across the Red Sea. But how? ....

Praise the Lord. We are all safe! What joy there is in the camp. Moses and his sister, Miriam, are leading us in a wonderful song of praise.

An amazing miracle has taken place. Moses stretched out his hand over the sea and a strong east wind came. All night it pushed the sea back until we could walk across on dry ground. As we crossed, there was a wall of water on each side of us!

But the Egyptians weren't that far behind. God sent confusion to their army. Wheels came off their chariots and they couldn't drive them properly. When the last of us reached the other side. Moses stretched out his hand over the water and it flooded back. All the soldiers and horsemen have been killed.

Joshua

Dear Diary,

We had been walking in the hot dusty desert for three days and had not found any water. We were tired and thirsty. When we did find water it was bitter and undrinkable. Everyone started making a fuss.

But God showed Moses a piece of wood, and when he threw it into the water the bitter taste disappeared. How refreshing to drink this cool liquid.

We are camping at a place called Elim. There are twelve springs and seventy palm trees here. What a relief to rest in the shade and to bathe in cool waters.

But two months after we left Egypt our people have begun to grumble because they are hungry. Some wish they were in Egypt. However, God has miraculously given us food. Last night, some quail flew onto the camp. We rushed out to catch them, and were soon preparing tasty meals.

Early this morning flakes appeared on the desert floor. We didn't know what they were. 'It's food,' said Moses. We're to collect as much as we need but are not to keep any of it overnight. More will come each day. Only on the day before our Sabbath rest are we to collect enough for two days.

Our bread from heaven is called 'manna', and it tastes like wafers made from honey.

Joshua

Dear Diary,

Moses was in despair today. Our water supply had run out, and it was a surprise to hear loud voices demanding some more. A quarrel with Moses broke out and the people nearly stoned him.

God told Moses to take some of our leaders to a rock at Horeb. When he hit it with his stick, water came out and there was enough for everyone! The place is called 'Massah' (testing) because the Lord was tested there.

But that wasn't our only problem ... Our enemies, the Amalekites attacked us. I chose some men to fight them and then we went to battle. What a battle! Moses, Aaron and Hur went up on a hill. While Moses held up his hands we won the battle, but when he lowered them we began to lose. Moses' arms grew tired, so Aaron and Hur held them up. They stayed steady until sunset and – praise God – we won a great victory!

Joshua

Dear Diary,

It is three months since we left Egypt. We are camping in front of Mount Sinai. The people have been excited about meeting with God … and today was the day!

It was awesome to wake to the sound of rumbling thunder. I saw great flashes of lightning. Thick cloud hung over the mountain. Then, the sound of a loud trumpet blasted through the camp. How we trembled. Moses led us to the bottom of the mountain. It was covered with smoke. What happened next fills me with awe, for our Lord came down in fire. The whole mountain trembled violently; the trumpet blasts became louder, and Moses spoke with God. Our people were terrified and thought that if God spoke to them they would die.

Moses is still on the mountain with God. The people have returned to the camp in fear and wonder.

Joshua

Dear Diary,

Moses and I were walking towards our Israelite camp today. Moses had been on Mount Sinai, and God had given him ten commandments (laws) on tablets of stone.

As we came closer, we heard the people shouting wildly. My heart sank when I saw what was happening. Aaron and the people had melted jewellery and made a golden calf. A huge party was underway. They were dancing and worshipping the calf god.

Moses was so angry that he threw the tablets to the ground, smashing them to pieces. Aaron had let everyone get out of control.

Our people thought Moses might not come back, and they wanted other gods to help them. How could they think that a lump of gold would guide them? God is very angry.

Joshua

P.S. Moses has burned the calf and ground it to powder. He is now pleading for God's forgiveness.

Dear Diary,

We are still at Sinai. God told Moses to chisel out two stone tablets like the first ones and to go back up the mountain. No one was allowed to go with him, or be seen anywhere on the mountain. Not even the herds were to graze in front of it.

When Moses came back I could see his face shining brightly – it was so bright no one would go near him – not even Aaron. What a holy God we worship!

Moses called us over, and, though his face was still dazzling, we made our way to him. He gave us the ten laws which God had given him, and then covered his face with a veil.

Whenever Moses speaks with God he takes off the veil, but afterwards his face is so bright that he has to cover it again.

Joshua

Dear Diary,

Moses chose me to go on a special mission. With eleven other men I went to spy on the land of Canaan, the land God has promised to give to us.

When we returned from this mission I had so much to tell the people. The land is truly a land flowing with milk and honey. The fruit is plentiful and oh, so juicy! One cluster of grapes was so big we had to carry it between two of us – slung over a pole.

But some of the other spies did not think we could live there. They disagreed with me and with Caleb, one of the other spies. The people listened to the other spies and not to us. The other spies told them about the giants and strong cities in Canaan. They should have trusted in God to help them but they did not. They refused to believe God's promise.

Moses and Aaron fell face down in front of us all. Caleb and I tore our clothes and pleaded with the people but they wouldn't listen.

God is angry with the people and is punishing us. No one over the age of twenty will be allowed to live in Canaan except for Caleb and me.

Joshua

Dear Diary,

There has been a rebellion. Korah, Dathan and Abiram joined with 250 leaders and accused Moses of making himself too important. Moses told Korah and his followers to meet Aaron and himself in order to prove that Moses is God's chosen leader.

Everyone was told to move away from the tents of Korah, Dathan and Abirim. Then Moses spoke, 'If the earth opens up and swallows them, you will know that they have treated God without respect.' At that moment, the ground swallowed them up! Then, fire came down on the 250 leaders and they all died. What a terrible end for people who should have known better.

Some time after that Aaron and Moses both died. Aaron's son, Eleazer, took his place. God's instructions were that I should replace Moses. When Moses died I was filled with sadness but I quickly sent two spies to look at the Promised Land again. They are back safely and they say that everyone there is afraid of us.

A woman called Rahab took the spies into her home. She hid them under some flax on her roof. She told the king that the spies had left, and he sent men to chase them. Rahab's kindness will be rewarded. She will tie a red cord in her window and all those in her house will be saved when we attack the city.

Joshua

Dear Diary,

God promised that he will cause our people to respect me, just as with Moses. This is how he kept his promise ...

We crossed the River Jordan on dry ground. First God commanded the priests who carry the ark of the covenant to stand in the Jordan. The water was very high, but as soon as they stepped in, it stopped flowing.

God commanded one man from each of the twelve tribes to pick up a stone from the river bed. These were piled up in memory of what God had done. When everyone had crossed and the priests and the ark came out of the river, the water rushed back. Now everyone knows that God is powerful.

Joshua

Dear Diary,

Jericho is a strong city … or perhaps I should say was. It had great walls – hard to attack. But God helped us. God instructed that our armed men must march around the city once a day for six days. Seven priests were to blow trumpets of rams' horns. And then on day seven we were to march around Jericho seven times. The priests were then to blow their trumpets and everyone give a loud shout. God's promise was that the walls of Jericho would fall down.

This is exactly what happened.

God kept his promise. The walls of Jericho are in ruins. The city is ours. Only Rahab and her family have been saved. God taught me many things in the desert. Without a doubt he is a faithful and mighty God. He always keeps his promises.

Joshua

ISBN: 978-1-84550-792-3
Published in 1995, reprinted in 2012
Christian Focus Publications, Genies House
Fearn, Tain, Ross-shire, IV20 1TW, U.K.